On Home Ground

On Home Ground

ALAN LELCHUK

WITH ILLUSTRATIONS BY
MERLE NACHT

GULLIVER BOOKS
HARCOURT BRACE JOVANOVICH
San Diego   Austin   Orlando

HBJ

Requests for permission to make copies of
any part of the work should be mailed to:
Permissions, Harcourt Brace Jovanovich, Publishers,
Orlando, Florida 32887.

Library of Congress Cataloging-in-Publication Data

Lelchuk, Alan.
On home ground.

"Gulliver books."
Summary: Set in Brooklyn in the wake of World War II,
and in the shadow of Ebbets Field, a young boy
is confronted with an emotional tangle of choices
that involves baseball, friendship, and family.
[1. Fathers and sons—Fiction.
2. Baseball—Fiction.
3. Brooklyn Dodgers (Baseball team)—Fiction.
4. Jews—Fiction.
5. Brooklyn (New York, N.Y.)—Fiction]
I. Nacht, Merle, ill. II. Title.
PZ7.L53733On 1987 [Fic] 87-8496
ISBN 0-15-200560-9

Designed by Michael Farmer
Printed in the United States of America
First edition
A B C D E

To Saul at four, almost a fan

ADULT BOOKS BY ALAN LELCHUK

American Mischief
Miriam at Thirty-four
Shrinking
Miriam in Her Forties

On Home Ground

IN THE SPRING of 1947, when I was nine and a half, Burt began taking me to the ball games. You know, the real thing, the Dodger games, back when they played in Brooklyn. Burt was about twenty-two, tall, light, firm. He lived on the third floor of our apartment house in the Brownsville section of Brooklyn, and ever since I could remember, he had been like a big brother to me. (Just as Sally, his bun-haired mother, had been the grandmother I had never had, rocking me to sleep with lullabies in Yiddish and Polish in her fabric shop downstairs on Sutter Avenue.) When I was six, Burt had helped me construct a miniature railroad station. Sitting on the floor in our living room, working with bits of smooth, unfinished woods, we built it together, which always disturbed my father for some reason.

And when Burt left college to join the air force in 1942 to become a pilot, he became a real-life hero to me, like my radio gods Frank Merriwell and Tom Mix. The fact that his B-17 bomber was shot down over Germany and Burt pronounced "missing in action" for six months before being confirmed as a "prisoner of war"—phrases that attacked my heart—only added to his heroic aura. When he returned home in 1945, limping, thin, pale, but sporting a full mustache, it was as much a homecoming for me as for him. As he grabbed me in his arms and swung me high and wide, embracing me in the crackling leather aviator jacket and white silk scarf, I felt like I was rotating on a Ferris wheel, spinning with dizzying delight.

He surprised me with my own pair of first-lieutenant bars, which I put under my pillow that night and checked first thing every morning after that.

Brooklyn in the late forties, though the largest of New York's five boroughs, was a small town made up of many different neighborhoods and peoples, who respected the separate territories and mostly ran into each other at school sports events. In Greenpoint lived the Irish; in Flatbush or Coney Island, the secular Jews; in Williamsburg, the Hasidic and ultra-Orthodox Jews; in Bay Ridge, the Italians; in Bedford Stuyvesant, the blacks; and in some sections, like Brownsville, a mix of Jews and blacks. And everywhere there bloomed, like tulips in spring, lovely parks and large shade trees, thanks to the Dutch who had settled there more than three hundred years before. We lived on the border between tidy East Flatbush and hungry Brownsville, the boundary marked by the IRT El subway line that ran above East 98th Street. Mine was a bustling, cheerful neighborhood of small, busy shops and brick apartment buildings, with a sprinkling of two-family homes. Just as any country boy knew every inch of his dirt road or meadow, so I knew every crooked brick and crocodile crack in my sidewalks. The clang of the electric trolley cars on Ralph Avenue and the thunder of the overhead subway were, for me, a kind of outdoor music. And I felt at home in the shops on Sutter Avenue, like Rosie's Variety Store where I bought my pink spaldeens (nineteen cents apiece) for punchball and stickball, or Julius's Jewelry Shop where Julie from England and his pale spinster sister served tea at four o'clock each afternoon and let me peer through their jeweler's loupe at intricate wrist-watch mechanisms. At the corner Woolworth Five and Dime, amid the dark walnut counters, my pals and I roamed the wide aisles in search of new booty to long for and to save up our pennies and nickels for. Egg creams and lime rickeys were the best drinks, for sure, and on a hot summer day there was nothing more delicious than creamy orange Popsicles or dripping chocolate Fudgsicles. And I could tell you right off the perfect sites for playing ball, our favorite pastime—the PS 189 schoolyard for softball, the Lincoln Terrace grass field for hardball, the vacant lot on Ralph Avenue for punchball, and the stone steps of Alan Bloom's two-family home for stoop-ball. Maybe the best thing about our neighborhood was the number of kids who lived right there. On our block alone there may have been twenty-five or thirty who hung around after school and dinner toss-ing balls, cradling mitts, taking practice swings, ready to play anything, or—at any time—ready to go uptown on the IRT and for sixty cents sit in the bleachers and cheer for our beloved Dodgers. Who would want to grow up anywhere else?

Anyway, Burt started taking me to the ballpark during that spring of '47. After I got permission to leave early from my fourth-grade teacher, Miss Gidden, who favored me because among other things I was so quick to learn her unconventional way of doing long division (we dropped numbers into oblong circles drawn with chalk on the blackboard), Burt would meet me at two o'clock in front of PS 189 on Rockaway Parkway twice a week. We either drove up to Ebbets Field in his ratty Nash coupe or hailed a taxi to the Utica Avenue subway stop, took the IRT uptown three stops to Franklin Avenue, and walked from there. Passing the Botanical Gardens, we sometimes could hear the crowd shouting from the field, and Burt would squeeze my hand and wink at me. Excited, I'd wink back and pick up his swifter pace, half-worrying that he was going too fast for his own good.

You see, the reason for Burt's idle freedom was

his war wound. While trying to escape from a Nazi prison camp, he had been shot with experimental glass bullets—like the Lone Ranger's silver bullets, I associated—that had deposited thousands of glass shards throughout his body. Now he was undergoing a seemingly unending series of surgeries to remove the largest and most painful pieces, with time in between given over to recovery and school. He had returned to New York University in Manhattan, attending classes three or four mornings a week, and was studying for a degree in engineering.

Naturally, on these treks to the ballpark, Burt wore his khaki service uniform, complete with Purple Heart, and we'd enter free via a designated turnstile. And because we went on weekdays for the most part, it frequently happened that the red-jacketed grandstand ushers, sighting Burt and me and some empty box seats, waved us down from the lower grandstand. Like passing through our own "Open Sesame," we were suddenly transported to another world, greener and more magical, seated in boxes along the first baseline, just up from the Brooklyn dugout. Being so close to the field, where you heard the crack of the Louisville slugger slugging a line drive and the smack of the baseball pegged into the first baseman's glove, scooped my heart with pleasure. When Burt tried to tip the ushers for their kindness, they would instead tip their caps and sometimes even pat Burt's shoulder, in gratitude for his service.

Our seats had an extra attraction that spring. The Bums, our Dodgers, had brought up a special rookie to play first base. I mean, he was special aside from his smart hitting, clutch fielding, and fierce running. He was special because the color of his skin was dark, darker than our mahogany bureau, and emphatically stood out in bold relief against the soft white flannel of the Dodger uniform. And because he was surrounded by all those white players, he was like some kind of black orchid set in a field of regular white daisies. When I described it that way to Burt, he charged, "You've been sneaking into the Botanical Gardens again, haven't you?" (Well, he was right, actually.)

Indeed, all the newspapers, like the *New York Post*, the *Daily News*, and the *Times*, had been filled with stories and pictures of Jackie Robinson's "historic signing" by Branch Rickey, the brave Brooklyn owner. The picture I liked best showed bespectacled Mr. Rickey pretending to have slapped Robby's cheek, and the player turning to offer the other one, dramatizing his response to the coming racist attacks. After all, he was the first Negro to be given a shot in the big leagues, and how he performed, how he carried himself, would determine the future of black men in baseball—or even whether there was to be a future for them. Mr. Rickey, as always, had done the shrewd thing, first by picking Jackie, who was as unusual a man as he was a player, and then by seasoning him for a year in Triple A at Montreal. For here, in the majors, the pressures were sure to be terrific. "I pity the poor bastard," remarked a Dodger teammate. "This is not the Negro leagues, but the majors, and he's gonna be thrown to all the white wolves, umps included! I sure hope he's no ordinary fellow."

That Jackie Robinson was no ordinary fellow, in any sense, was apparent the second time we watched him play that spring. The Cardinals were in town

for a three-game series, the same feared Redbirds—
of course a real fan knew every team nickname—
who had won the pennant the year before, beating
out our beloved Bums. These Cards were considered
the most "southern" club in the league, southern in
temperament as well as in player origin. At the time,
I wasn't too sure what that meant, because when I
looked at St. Louis on a map, all I saw was that it
was west of the Mississippi, the only team that far
west. It was so far, in fact, that Red Barber and
Connie Desmond had to report the games via the
Morse code of a ticker tape. Huddled by my Philco
radio late into the Brooklyn night, I held on to their
every word, listening as a triple on tape often turned
into a phrase like poetry, except it wasn't gushy.
"There's a long drive into the pea patches of left
center," Red would exclaim, and I'd be carried a
long way, too, away from the city and my bedroom,
to some far-off country of farms and dreams.

We arrived in the fourth inning and had barely
taken our seats when the first strange thing occurred.
Country Slaughter, the Cards' hustling outfielder,
hit a slow grounder to second, where Eddie Stanky

fielded it and threw a routine peg to Robinson at first to get the runner. He did, but at the same time Slaughter got Robby, slashing his planted foot with his spikes as he crossed the bag. *Cheap shot!* Jackie sank to the ground, twisting in pain, grasping the foot. Leisurely, Slaughter jogged off the field, making sure to pass near Robby and flash him a little smile and nod. Welcome to the Big White Leagues, I read the gesture.

"Did you see that?" I asked Burt, my voice raised.

He nodded and watched.

The crowd was stunned, and so, it seemed, were the players. Only Pee Wee Reese, the shortstop, came over to Jackie and helped him up. But as he walked the hobbling Robinson around, to assess the injury and maybe shake it off, I saw that I was wrong; the other players were not so much stunned or angry as . . . uninterested, sort of detached. They turned away from the pair, looking instead at the ground or up at the stands. *The rats!*

Well, Robby, after refusing to come out of the game, got back into position. Just then, however, a

pitch-black cat was tossed onto the field from the Cardinal dugout, and she scatted across the infield. I saw the plate umpire take off his mask and smile with amusement. And from the Cards' side someone called, "Go cry to your brother, little Sambo!"

If that wasn't enough to pump my blood, we then heard "Yeah, beat it, black boy!" hurled from the Brooklyn dugout, aimed at the caller's own teammate.

What a crazy betrayal, I thought. Burt, sensing my confusion and rage, put a hand on my arm.

All the subtle beauty of baseball's routine was interrupted by this new tension. Gradually, I tried to get back into the scoring of the game and the familiar codes like 6-3, FO, K, 5-4-3 DP (numbers almost as secret as my Captain Midnight code).

More peculiar stuff erupted in the bottom of the next inning when Robinson came up to bat against Red Munger, the Cards' hard fastballer. Until then, Munger had shown fine control, but now, against Robby, after two easy outs, he threw two high hard ones right at his head, decking him. Not a word of protest came from the Dodger bench, and I realized that Robinson was fighting it alone—even his teammates, except Pee Wee, were his enemies. Hardly a ripple rose from the crowd. Everyone seemed to be waiting, watching, before voicing their sentiments or votes. Jackie picked himself up, looked momentarily at the catcher, who obviously had said something, and stood back in, cocking his bat high . . . though not as high as the tension that was in the air right then. An extension of the field, the crowd remained alarmingly quiet.

The next pitch was the predictable wasted curve, outside and low, and Robby let it pass. Then Munger tried another curve, this one maybe catching the corner. Suddenly, Robinson laid out his bat horizontally and lay down a dainty bunt along the first baseline, surprising everyone. The bunt was just slow enough for the pitcher to have to cover it, and Munger came over. And there was Jackie, almost jogging, timing perfectly the pitcher's run from the mound and his own revenge. Picking up his pace, he crashed into Munger, sending him flying. Robinson didn't look back as he jogged into first. For the first time that day, the crowd clapped. I was yelling.

"Hey, *boy*," called out one of the players attending to the pitcher, "you're through!"

"You uppity niggah!" came openly from another player.

Robby stood on first, stony, ebony, hands on hips.

While the names and epithets continued, a voice from the Dodger bench called out, "Attaway, Jackie."

Burt tapped my arm. "He's got the guts, hasn't he?"

I nodded, entranced by the incident, the man.

"Does he have the talent to match his guts?" Burt wondered aloud.

Robby danced off first, but the next hitter swung at the first pitch and popped out, ending the inning.

The game settled down into a pitcher's duel, with Munger outdueling little Vic Lombardi 2-1, and with no more incidents around first due to Robinson's quick eye and fast foot off the bag. In the home half of the seventh, with the good lady Gladys Gooding serenading us on the organ—only at Ebbets Field and Fenway Park—and the crowd calling for a rally, Robby came up again.

"He walks like he's in pain," I noted. "Do you think it's still the foot?"

"I think maybe he just walks that way," Burt answered.

Robinson tapped dirt from his spikes and stood in, holding the bat high, deflecting the names hurled at him. He waited, as we did, but there were no knockdown pitches this time. Showing patience and quick wrists, Jackie, at the last instant, fouled off several fine pitches and finally drew a walk. Down to first in that odd, pigeon-toed trot, he looked awkward, misfit; a penguin, not a runner.

There was one out, with Pee Wee the batter, and Jackie slowly extended his lead off first.

"Gee, will he go?"

"Could be," said Burt. "He sure does get out there."

Baseball's changing time stood almost still, suspended now. While Reese waited at the plate, Munger went into his stretch and looked around, and Jackie started to do his dangling dance, about ten to twelve feet from the bag. Hands stretched out loosely at his sides, crouching like the halfback he had been at UCLA, Jackie jiggled this way and that, forcing Munger to throw over to first three times, step off the mound, then throw again, almost wildly. Each time, Robinson was back to first easily.

The count was full, Munger threw over a few more times, then pitched, and Robinson ran. Pee Wee, not getting around fast enough, hit a setup two-bouncer to second, where Schoendienst fielded it smoothly, but having no chance to double up the already-running Jackie, pegged to first. Pee Wee was out by a half dozen steps.

Robinson was *still* running, however. He had gone into second as though to stop, of course, and then, incredibly, just as Schoendienst began his throw, Robinson shifted into high gear and propelled toward third. By the time that Musial at first realized what was happening, Robinson was three-quarters of the way there, and Musial's throw was a half second late. Musial stood with his hands on his hips, staring in disbelief. Schoendienst looked down at the ground. Marion, the shortstop, picked up a few pebbles and tossed them away. The great Cardinal

infield was shocked. Jackie had already dusted himself off and was standing upright on third, hands on
hips. His dark face showed no expression, though
he had just taken two bases on a groundout!

Now two voices cheered him from his own dugout.

Burt looked over at me and winked. "Ever seen
that before?"

I shook my head. "No, sir!"

"And not against the St. Louis Cardinals, Aaron."

There were two outs now, and Jackie was on
third—still not much hope. The batter was Bruce
Edwards, a right-handed hitter who had not done
much against Munger.

Once again, Robinson drifted off the bag, extending
his lead. The pitcher, after consulting with Ku-
rowski, the third baseman, and Marion, the short-
stop, decided to work from a stretch, holding his
windup for a full second.

That didn't daunt Jackie in the least. Now about
sixty feet from home and facing Munger from a
shorter distance, Robby began to edge out for that
same outrageously long lead and jiggle. And as soon

as the pitcher threw to the plate, he raced halfway home—exhilarating, terrifying, everyone.

"He's shameless, too, on top of everything else," marveled Burt.

I didn't fully know what that meant, but I was too excited to inquire. Hoping against hope, I crossed my fingers under my legs and stroked my blue Dodger cap three times for luck.

On the fourth pitch to the batter, Jackie again darted for home. But this time he didn't stop and hold up. He kept running! The ball was low and outside. Jackie hookslid into the third-base side of the rubber plate, creating a circle of sand cloud, and the ump put his hands down wide and flat. *Safe!* We were all standing, cheering him, as he trotted in. At the dugout, Reese, the manager, and a third player greeted him for his daring skill.

"They gotta get used to him, don't you think?" I asked.

"They better hurry," Burt said.

The Dodgers won in the ninth, 3-2, and moved into first place.

PERIODICALLY THEN, a few times a week during April and May when the Dodgers were at home, we went up to Ebbets Field to watch them play. Brooklyn continued to lead in a tight race, and the team's pennant chances were the subject dearest to our schoolboy hearts. In classrooms and school-yards, on street corners and ballfields, during street games of ring-a-levio and Johnny-on-the-pony, we fought and argued like crazy with our New York rivals—the Giant and Yankee followers. "C'mon, where's their pitching?" they'd ask. Or, "Do you really think they can win once the Cards start hit-ting?" And, "Jackie'll never hold up; they'll break him for sure. Wait till August!" was a favorite of theirs.

You see, there was something special about the relationship between the Dodgers and Brooklyn. They were a tight part of us, and we—the fans—a part of them. To the rest of the country we were a kind of family joke. It was reflected in the movies, in the songs, on the radio. The joke was all in good fun, but a joke nevertheless. If you came from Brooklyn, that was supposed to mean you were sort of queer and daffy, just as the old 1930s Dodgers had been. That's how they had earned their nickname, "the Bums," in the first place. They were also considered unlucky, maybe even cursed. Well, there *was* the time that Mickey Owens, our fine catcher, dropped a third strike with two out in the ninth inning of a world series game in 1941, and we went on to lose the game and the series. The way *Sport* magazine saw it, their fate was our fate—no matter how queer and unlucky it happened to be.

And now, once again, we were doing something odd, something different. . . . We had a black man playing major-league ball for us. Only this time, maybe it wasn't that funny, maybe we were going too far? The grown-ups seemed to wonder. But we, the kids, knew something else. We knew that we were now going to get our revenge on the rest of the league, and perhaps on the whole country, as well. This time, our screwy judgment and peculiar ways were going to be *their* bad luck. We felt it in our blood. And, if we won, maybe even the whole darn country would come around to seeing things our way for a change.

Jackie, and what happened to him that summer, was also our special treat. He remained the object of everyone's attention—players and fans. The same pattern we had witnessed in that first series emerged again and again. Teams taunted him at every opportunity, trying to slash his body and unsettle his mind. His teammates seemed to be taking sides, for and against, and the umps continued to turn away when things got hot. Except for Pee Wee, it appeared he was on his own and forced to remember Mr. Rickey's chief warning: "Turn the other cheek, Jack, or you'll never last." Using just his skills and brains, with defiant baseball acts doing all his talking, Jackie had to handle the ordeal, the challenge. He reminded me a little of the scout Natty Bumppo, my hero from Classic Comics. Both were alone and gutsy in dangerous territory.

Jackie seemed to learn very quickly the other teams' vulnerable points—sloppy infielders, big-windup pitchers, reckless catchers, loose cutoff teams—and push toward their breaking points. It was almost as though he toyed with them, in a kind of cat-and-mouse game, which infuriated them all the more.

For me, almost ten but already a true fan for two years, it was a new and exciting time. I, too, felt like a rookie. The only really bad moments came when, on occasion, I'd hear a muffled moan at my side, and glancing over, see Burt gasping, his face ashen white. I knew that his stitches were pulling, or that bits of glass were cutting him somewhere inside. At those times all the splendid sights and sounds of a ballpark in spring would be eclipsed. And Burt, seeing me fearful and at a loss, and aware that his pained state was shattering my Cracker Jack glee, would ask me to get him some water. By the time I arrived back, he'd be calm again, the cloud of darkness over and gone. His wink then would pull strongly at my affections, and sometimes I'd even hug him, for reasons I wasn't sure of. And it would be a few minutes before I could return my concentration to baseball rapture.

⸺

MY FATHER, a short, powerful man from Russia, felt about Burt the way he did about America—he was never quite at home with either. Both men were pretty stubborn and conceited, especially when together, and were merely polite to one another whenever they met.

Papa always gave the impression that he didn't fully believe Burt's injury, that Burt was imagining more than what was real. Though my father never said it outright, he'd cock his head to the side and raise his eyebrows. Burt thought my father was a "greenhorn" and "Commie"—which probably was true—and he resented that. By "greenhorn" he meant "immigrant," of course. My father had left Russia during the chaos of 1917, when his own father had been killed and the family had decided to send him, their youngest son, to America to seek his fortune. They had meant for him to return, and I always felt my father had one foot in each country. By "Commie," Burt explained, he meant that Father still believed strongly in Joseph Stalin and his Bolshevik policies. I felt somehow ashamed of Father for this belief, as though it were dirty, and did my best to conceal it from my friends and their parents whenever the subject of politics came up. I would speak, instead, of the letter he had received from President

Franklin Delano Roosevelt. Framed and hung on our foyer wall, it praised Papa for his service as head of the Brownsville Air Raid Wardens. But that didn't keep the nosy parents from occasionally making little jokes about my "leftie" father, jokes that made me squirm with discomfort and strange feelings.

On the other hand, my father believed that the Breams, who were also immigrants, had spoiled Burt, and that he was an opinionated smart aleck made even more difficult by the air force and college. My father and Burt made a curious pair in looks, too, one a balding, stocky European gentleman who always dressed formally, and the other a tall, slender, brown-haired young man, casual in dungarees, and now sporting a fine, mature mustache. Probably because of Burt and my father, I came to believe that we Americans felt easier in jeans and sports shirts, while Europeans preferred dressy duds, with neckties and all.

Anyway, my father did not approve of our long, intimate friendship and my total devotion to Burt. Even when I was six and Burt was helping me construct that miniature railroad and depot—the ongoing pleasure of my early years—my father would sneer at the two of us as we built and invented, sprawled out on the shabby old rug. Although I didn't fully comprehend his animosity toward Burt— was it jealousy of *him?* Of his closeness to me? Perhaps of his family's closeness to my mother?—I knew enough to want to keep the two of them apart and keep my special friendship more and more private. It was strange how complicated things seemed to be among us and how hard I had to work to make sure that things flowed smoothly all around.

I was, therefore, not happy to discover one evening at dinner that my father had somehow heard about my Ebbets Field journeys with Burt.

Eating the *plate flanken,* or boiled meat, and potatoes that he salted heavily and adored (and I despised), he began questioning me, almost slyly, about the trips.

"So you've been going to the baseball games all spring, eh?"

"Well, not exactly."

"And tell me, did you skip school, too, to do this?" he asked, staring at me.

"Of course not, Papa." And I explained how I had carefully gotten permission from my teacher.

"I see," he commented, slowly slicing a piece of seeded rye bread. Then the prosecutor, prying almost innocently, asked, "Did your mother help you in all this? She agreed, right?"

I squirmed in my stiff chair and tried to appease him by applying the dreaded salt, too.

The widening eyes and tightening forehead belied his benevolent tone.

"No," I managed, only a half-lie.

The small brown eyes flared, and the pale oval face grew alert with anger. "From now on, you'll attend to school and forget that *narrishkeit*." Foolishness, a word I knew well. "And you can tell your friend that, too." He chewed his rye with gusto.

"But, Papa, please, they're fighting for first, and Robinson—"

He took my small wrist and held it firmly, staring at me. Quietly he commanded, "You'll stay in school until *three* o'clock and only then leave. And if—"

Just then my mother reentered the room, unaware of the discussion he had begun after she had left. A trim, lively woman in her forties, with auburn hair and hazel eyes, she had become my protector as soon as I was old enough—five, six?—for Papa to turn stern toward me.

As she sat down at the wooden kitchen table, my father shook his head in disdain. "*Bist du klug,*" he said, "*very* smart."

"What are you talking about?"

"Baseball instead of school, that's what. Very nice. What do you care if he grows up to be a truck driver?"

"Aah, stop it, will you? When he stops getting A's, then I'll worry." Her forehead creased with lines of familiar fatigue from such battles.

"Well, no more playing hooky with Mister Burt."

"Are you crazy?" she responded. "What are you saying? No one played hooky."

"I suppose you skipped Hebrew school, too, now and then? Well, no more. No more baseball until school is finished."

"Oh, yeah?" I couldn't help challenging him at last.

He looked at me with excitement, his fury mounting and driving him with a theatrical power.

"Aaron, sshhh. You let me handle it, all right?" my mother urged, knowing the harsh consequences of my direct rebellion.

I held my tongue and scraped my fingernail along the oilcloth covering the table.

My father seemed to sigh with disappointment at the thwarted fight and returned to his boiled meat. "To soccer games he won't come, but to baseball. Eh." He shook his head.

Yes, it had been stupid of me not to accompany him the last time a European all-star team had visited Ebbets Field to play an exhibition match. But *soccer?* Once I went with him, knew none of the players, had no team to cheer for, and was bored. Not again. . . . I was already beginning my strategy of going to the Dodger games on the sly, unbeknown even to my mother, so she wouldn't—couldn't—be held accountable. He could slap me around, but his attacks on her turned me inside out.

MISS GIDDEN sat in her special high chair, propped up with a pillow because of her diminutive height. Her little feet, encased in black bunion shoes, dangled between the rungs as she nibbled at her chicken leg. Kids around the school thought she was a kook for doing such a thing in class, but I didn't mind much. She had eccentric habits, and that was all right with me. Slow Heshy was at the blackboard, trying to figure out how to get through a long-division problem Miss Gidden had just put to him. Outside I could hear some kids playing punchball in the schoolyard at recess, and I checked my watch; just fifteen minutes to go. Then I'd silently grab my jacket from the wardrobe and be on my way downstairs, making sure to avoid Mr. Richman, the principal, which was part of my agreement with Miss Gidden. Carefully, I began to write out the Dodger and Brave lineups for the day, including the starting pitchers. The Braves were the second toughest team in the league, and there was just no way I was going

to miss this series, or for that matter, any other—
no matter what *he'd* do to me if he ever found
out. In the back of my hardback composition note-
book I printed the names precisely: Ryan, Torge-
son, Holmes, Elliot . . . and I tried to remember
whether Sain or Spahn was opening the series for
the Braves.

"Aaron, didn't you hear me?" The sharp, nasal
voice broke into my thoughts. "Can you help out
our friend here?"

I looked up and saw that Miss Gidden was beck-
oning me, as she commonly did, especially on a
shortened afternoon. Quickly, I got up and hustled
to the blackboard as though I had been studying the
equation all along. Actually, I liked it up there. White
chalk in hand, I'd erase some dodo's blundering chaos
and put neat order into all those numbers. I felt as
cozy in the classroom as I did at the ball game. I
looked at the problem, pretending to reflect upon
its difficulty before solving it. Neither Miss Gidden
nor I wanted the class to think I was getting spoiled
by her concession to me for baseball. Finally, I began
scribbling away, making sure not to squeak but al-

ready sighting Jackie taking his big lead off first. *Boy, that would be rough against those Boston hurlers!*

"Thank you, Aaron," she said when I was finished, her rimless eyeglasses reflecting light from the large windows.

And in ten minutes I was gone from the room, flying outside into the warm, free, sunshiny day. Burt was already there, and I got into the Checker cab.

"You're sure you want to go through with this?" He looked at me. "If your father finds out, he'll be pretty upset."

"I know. But he won't find out—unless *you* tell him," I kidded.

"Oh, I just may forget to," he said, tapping my shoulder.

As we took off, I imagined our journey as some sort of air force mission, maybe like one of Burt's B-17 flights over Germany. I tried on his soft military cap with the gold bars on it to see if it fit yet. *We're going somewhere secret, doing something dangerous,* I thought. The cap flopped down over my forehead, and I handed it back to him.

And later, the game didn't disappoint, though we didn't win. Sain beat the Bums 2-1 with his endless variety of curveballs—throwing sidearm, overhead, fast and slow. (Burt had described one overhead curve as "a white apple rolling off a tabletop, with maybe a two-foot drop.") And though Jackie had managed to turn a single into a hustling double, Sain had almost picked him off second, a close call.

"Jackie'll get to know him the second time around, huh?" I wondered out loud.

"Well," Burt answered, "some pitchers stay pretty tough, and you learn to take it easy with them. Sain and Spahn may be the two toughest."

The real fun came later, after the game, when Burt allowed me to wait outside the park with the other autograph hounds. When the players emerged, everyone raced to get to Carl Furillo and Ralph Branca, but I held back, hoping to get luckier. And sure enough, practically slipping through the parking lot the way he stole bases, there was Robinson. Carrying a blue gym bag, he moved in that now-familiar pigeon-walk fashion, as though he had needles stuck in his arches. It wasn't until I tried to catch up to him that I saw how rapidly he was moving. When I was within fifteen feet of him, I called out, "Jackie?" He turned, and I held up my scorecard. "May I have your autograph, Mr. Robinson?" My heart was beating rapidly—from my pace, from the moment.

Up close, his face was dark and stern. His expressive eyes were solemn as they fixed on me. For some reason, I didn't feel like a kid facing him, but older, more responsible. He asked my name, his voice surprisingly soft and gravelly. And as he wrote, "To Aaron," my blood leaped with excitement. He wrote on a slant, the letters small but legible, and when he looked up he asked if I was a ballplayer, too. "Sure," I blurted out, "but I'm mostly a Dodger fan. Especially of yours and Pee Wee's," I added. He examined me then, his high forehead visible, his black face a mask of . . . stubbornness, skepticism? I felt curiously at odds, afraid, maybe accused.

He turned to go, and I said something like, "Sain's tough, huh?"

For a second he seemed to relax and almost smiled. "Yes, he's a fine pitcher." With a small wave he was gone.

I was confused but high by the time I got back to Burt, and the emotion stayed with me the whole way home on the bumpy IRT. I held the scorecard like a private treasure, guarding it and peeking every now and then to make sure the autograph was still there. At one point, I looked across the aisle at a pale-faced man reading the *Daily News* and I saw, instead, the relentless ebony mask of Robinson facing me. I willed myself not to think any more about the day and tried to concentrate on making my five o'clock Hebrew school class. I didn't want to lie about *that* to Papa.

Leaving me at Sutter Avenue, Burt said, "Now don't lose that," referring to my prize, and I smiled. Then I raced like crazy to Topscott Street, where my Sholem Aleichem school was held in the basement of a two-family house.

We had a history lesson that day. But neither Moses nor the Jews he led through the wilderness could keep me from that daring double, the dark, stern face up close, or my perplexing excitement. I kept my scorecard beneath my green *Geschichte,* history, text on the slanted wood school desk and let my heart wander away from the words to those dropping white apples. Fortunately, though I was later called on twice to read sections of the Bible, my teacher, *Lehrer* Goichberg, suspected nothing as he conducted our small class of ten students, in Yiddish. Familiar with his ways, I was ready with a smile when he remarked about the "other Aaron," Moses' weak older brother, who got into such a mess when he allowed the children of Israel to forge and worship the golden calf while Moses was on Mount Sinai, receiving the Ten Commandments. My treasure secure, my mind on Robby and Pee Wee, I was ready for anything.

DINNER PASSED SMOOTHLY. My father asked me how Hebrew school went, and I was able to inform him truthfully. I couldn't resist putting in a good word for Goichberg, whom my father liked. I knew that Papa was considered a foolish "leftie" for sending me to the Socialist-sponsored Bund school, where students didn't have to wear yarmulkes, religion was unimportant, and the emphasis was on Yiddish, the daily worker's language. Most, if not all, the kids on the block went to a traditional Hebrew school, the Talmud Torah, where the holy language was taught, religious instruction was part of the curriculum, and the teacher-rebbes were despised. To our neighbors, all that happened in my Sholem Aleichem school—including being taught by a nonreligious teacher—was shameful, even blasphemous, and they were positive that I was learning how to grow up a Commie. Curiously enough, I was sympathetic to Papa's choice. I actually had a pretty good time at Hebrew school and admired Goichberg. Anyway, I finished eating as quickly as possible, helped dry the dishes and put them away for Mama (my nightly chore), and scooted downstairs. Carrying my prize, I anticipated the glory that awaited me at the evening punchball game.

We played on the vacant lot on Ralph Avenue that sat between Manny's Rug Store and Lloyd Brown's two-family house. It was a stony dirt lot,

maybe 150 feet in length and rather narrow. Home-plate was down at street level, which meant that when you punched the ball (you were supposed to use your knuckles, but Marty Davis slapped it with his open palm), you had to run uphill to the bases. Kids from other neighborhoods who played their punchball on smooth asphalt streets hated to play us there because of the crazy bounces and stony terrain. This made us love it all the more.

Although I was usually a sure-handed third base-man, that evening the pink rubber ball eluded my grasp, and I made several easy errors. My focus lay elsewhere. Mel Goldstein, a solid fielder who could be counted on to play a good game at either short-stop or middle position, sensed something was up and asked whether I was feeling sick or something.

The game ended just before dark and, as was our habit, we gathered at the standup mailbox on the corner of Ralph and Sutter, our social center. The Sutter Theater, only steps away, was showing *Double Indemnity,* a movie we were planning to see at our usual Saturday matinee. Diagonally across the street, a few hundred yards away, the New Lots IRT rumbled in and out on the overhead El. The June evening was warm and most promising. As the older guys kidded with passing girls (especially those with tight shirts or short shorts), we boxed or wrestled with each other or argued about the pennant race. There were perhaps ten or fifteen of us hanging out on the corner, city cubs at play, awaiting the end of school and rooting for our favorite teams, as they led the two leagues.

"Forget the Dodgers," said Alan Kamph, a die-hard Yankee fan. "Come September, and they'll blow it!"

"Yeah, the Cards look pretty strong with Pollet and Brecheen healthy again," responded Ronald Tavel.

"And don't forget 'Spahn and Sain and two days of rain,'" sang scholarly Jerry Fromm.

"Aah, Brooklyn'll murder those guys," asserted Ronnie Friedler, the beefy Dodger fanatic and neighborhood bully.

"Well, they didn't murder them today," I put in modestly. "In fact, they looked pretty feeble against Sain."

"Don't tell me you went again, Schlossy!" cried

Mel. Standing with hands on hips, he looked at me with open envy.

And then I began, slowly, to explain what the day had been like—how Sain had toyed with them and used his cunning kick and pickoff move; how Pistol Pete Reiser had almost cracked his head again lunging for a Holmes double; what the dropping white curves had looked like from behind the plate. I was deluged with the usual questions: Where'd we sit, did any foul balls come within our grasp, did I manage to get any autographs?

"Just one," I spoke coolly.

"Oh, yeah? Who?"

"Arkie Vaughan?" offered Steve Werter sarcastically, making the kids snicker by his reference to a minor player.

I paused theatrically. "Robinson."

"Who you joshin'?"

"I don't believe it," chipped in Stewie.

"C'mon, let's see it," said slender Kamph, who always reddened with excitement.

Instantly, I was encircled by a jury of twelve or

so, waiting to see the hard evidence. Carefully, slowly, I unrolled the scorecard and produced the proof they sought.

"Wow!"

"Holy moly!"

"Let's see that," ordered Friedler, practically ripping the program from my hands and inspecting it up close. "If you're conning us . . ." he said, brandishing his thick fist. "We can check this out, you know."

"It's for real—I swear," I blurted out, already afraid of his secret spy network.

Gradually, as the truth of the signature slowly sank in, they began to take on a new attitude toward me. I was like some kind of hero, someone who had braved bayonets and trenches to secure this fortune.

"How'd ya do it?"

"Who'd ya know?"

"C'mon, Schlossy," pleaded Jerry, "what'd ya do?"

Well, the funniest thing was that I got so caught up in the heat of my newfound glory that I began to foolishly enlarge and exaggerate my feat. I told them how I ran after Reese's car and almost got hit by it, and how Jackie had given me a big smile, and how—

"Aaron."

The voice torpedoed my glory, stopped my story.

"Can I see you for a minute?"

"Hello, Mr. Schlossberg," Kampherballs greeted my father.

"Good evening, Alan," my father returned, cordial as ever.

"Did you see whose autograph he got at the game today?" Ronnie Friedler jumped in. The bully was especially friendly with my father. What could I say or do? The subway train thundered wildly into the Sutter Avenue station, and the little bulbs on the movie marquee were suddenly sizzling.

I bit down slowly on my tongue, not moving.

And now, surprisingly, the circle of kids spread apart, respectfully opening the way for me to welcome my father. But I felt my knees turn to rubber, and I wished my friends would continue to surround me, like a wagon train.

He wore his dark suit, tie, and fedora and smiled broadly to my pals. *Couldn't they see beneath the uniform?* Possessively, he took my arm and led me across the street crocodiled with the old trolley tracks. I remember wishing I could run and follow those tracks to the end of Brooklyn!

The bluish black veil of the evening descended on me as we made our way into the brick fortress of 701 Ralph Avenue. He led me through the thick iron doors, into the faded, yellowing lobby, and up to the steel stairs, where I held onto the cold metal banister with all my might.

"Hello, Mr. Schlossberg," whispered a shadow by the mailboxes below.

My father, taken aback by the unexpected voice and figure, stopped to peer. "Is that you, Joey?" he asked, retreating into formality. "Why, how are you?"

"Fine, thanks," Joey Zorn answered. He joined us on the steps and ruffled my hair. "How's the left fielder doing?"

"Okay," I mumbled, desperately wanting him to stay with me.

To my father, he said, "Someday you'll have to see Aaron play the outfield. He can really go get 'em."

He spoke with the absolute authority of a superior softball player. A lean, dark young man of sixteen, Joey had a great natural swing, and could hit a softball farther than most guys could hit a baseball. His father having deserted his family and mad wife years before, Joey had grown up with a series of transient men, always envying my permanent father.

"Can he?" Father asked politely, as he began to move me in the direction of our first-floor landing.

From the recessed darkness I called out weakly, "Joey?"

He turned at the stairwell, about to ascend, and asked, "What's up, Aaron?"

Papa put a subtle force to his grip on my hand, and I could only shake my head. As he fumbled for the key on his jiggling key chain and began to unlock the thick steel door, I felt like I was about to enter prison for a severe punishment. My heart and stomach astir, we proceeded inside the long, dark foyer. Strangely, the grave mask of Jackie reappeared then, comforting and terrifying me as it had when he signed my scorecard.

Papa sat me down at the kitchen table, cornering me between the window and the wall and leaving no escape. I prepared myself, my eyes stinging from my concentration, and awaited his words, his sentencing.

Still wearing his gray fedora, he began, "So, you disobeyed me. . . ."

All through the ordeal of hard, punishing slaps, I hardly heard his brutal words and demands. Instead, I found myself focusing on warmer times together. I recalled sitting by that same kitchen table, listening to Papa reconstruct his Russian home. On thin sheets of paper, he would make fine pencil drawings of his village home outside Minsk, in White Russia, which used to be Poland in the old days. An embroiderer and designer, he'd draw in and shade the grounds, stables and horses, and his own room. I used to love to sit on his lap—when I was four—and was entranced by his work and by the tales he told of his family while he drew. Sometimes his cheeks were still stubbly with beard from the long day, and I'd have him rub the little bristles against my smoothness, asking if I'd have to shave when

*I was a man. (And longing for the day!) The history of
his well-off family and their prosperous lumber business—
the servants and houses and horses and land—always
struck me like some exotic fairy tale. The part about grandfather Alexander's death was especially Arabian Nightish.
Zeyda had had his head lopped off by a wild cossack general
on horseback who had come to rob the house!*

"Did it really happen that way, Papa?" I'd ask.

"Of course, silly boy," he'd say. "Why not?"

*And I'd always think: If such terrible things occurred
there, why, then, do you prefer Russia to our country? But
while I wanted very much to see his grand home and horses,
and greatly missed meeting my grandfather and grandmother and five uncles and aunts, I was glad, very glad,
that I was an American boy.*

The slaps and threats and wrist-twistings made
me hate him, but somehow they couldn't erase
those other memories or feelings.

⫘

ON SUNDAY MORNING, several days later,
my father and I spent our usual few hours at the
Brownsville Air Raid Wardens Club on Union Street.

The storefront room was thick with cigar and cigarette smoke, and two dozen men sat at tables playing pinochle, chess, checkers, or just *kibbitzing*. Naturally, Papa had dressed me in my hated woolen knicker-suit, and he wore his blue serge suit and a tie. Against my will on that morning, I played chess, the game my father had taught me when I was five, and that I had started playing in the club a few years later. In between his card games, Papa would come over and check out my match, pretty much taking for granted my regular victories by then. However, in my game against Sam Schwebel, whom I knew I could beat easily, I made sure to lose my queen in a foolish bishop pin, shocking Sam and angering my father. I enjoyed watching his mouth react to my beginner's mistake and his head shake from side to side in dismay. Of course, he could and would do nothing, right there. Restraining his hot temper in front of all the members, he smiled like a diplomat.

Later, walking back along Sutter Avenue, he gripped my hand extra-tight and uttered his standard curse: "*Bist du a goy*. How could you lose to that . . . that nobody?" He stopped briefly to say hello to Phil from the deli and then, alone again, offered, "You'll be a truck driver after all."

But I didn't care anymore; I felt freer, stronger for my private deception and his lost honor.

The sun had broken through the hazy morning, and I was sorry I was not going to spend the afternoon playing ball rather than going uptown with him.

As we walked back to our apartment house to grab a quick lunch (and to change into my light gabardines, I hoped), I thought about the storm of the other evening, how it had passed, but how the insult and humiliation had stayed. If we had not forgiven each other—and I had made a pact with myself never to let that happen—we had at least arrived at a calmer time. Slapping force had returned to the wings, and father and son, the actors, went through their rehearsal quite routinely.

When we arrived at our building, clusters of parents and kids had taken up their customary Sunday posts—sitting on folding chairs or wooden fruit crates, playing boxball or checkers, reading the papers (never the thick *Times* that Papa read), talking, kidding around. The street traffic was lighter on Sundays, and in a way we all missed the trolleys, which by then had been replaced by buses. I missed watching the more nervy kids hitch rides on the back of the trolleys—latching on to a low railing and crouching outside until the conductor left—as the cars clanged past our door. Father was greeted politely by the neighbors, most of whom looked upon him as a kind of zoo creature—weird, comic, maybe dangerous if touched. Not only was he an outcast, a "red" or "leftie," but he was also such an odd fish, forever formal in his double-breasted suits and twice-a-day shaves. Forever European in his opinions and tastes (chess, soccer, Chaplin). Forever aloof and somehow superior. Despite myself, I felt a flow of sympathy for him at such moments, when he so amused, and perhaps confused, people.

Holding a *Sunday Mirror,* Mr. Tavel, his one crony, asked, "So Herschel, how goes it?"

My father nodded and answered, "Fine, why not? And you, you lazy good-for-nothing?"

Mr. Tavel, a hardworking bookkeeper with slumping shoulders and longish sideburns, made a so-so gesture with his hands. He replied, "Could be better."

"Hello, Harry," put in curly-haired Mr. Werter, looking up from infighting with his son, Steven, and laughing at the blows. "The boy here thinks I can still take his hardest shots!" he called, taking one just then.

My father, a boxing fan—which stemmed from his friendship with Harold Green, a middleweight who lived on our block—smiled. "Try him in those Golden Gloves, Louie."

"Are you kidding? They'd knock his block off."

"Oh, yeah?" cried out Steven, pounding away with both fists at the midsection of his laughing father.

I was secretly glad for all the tumult, which served to distract everyone from my tweed knicker-suit and stern Sunday duties.

We were about to turn into the entrance of our building when the heavy front door opened, and Burt, in soldier's uniform, emerged. With that soft cap that looked like a folded brown envelope and his new handball tan, he looked deceptively fit and splendidly youthful.

Naturally, he draped his arm around me and gave my father a correct hello.

My father nodded, a diagonal sort of nod, which I knew well. "So, are you off to Palestine to fight for Zionism, or have you given up that *narrishe* idea?" Foolish, again.

"No, not at all. First I have to take care of some unfinished business."

"This baseball business, you mean?"

Burt, slightly taller, eyed him directly. "More like college and hospitals, Harry."

"A Jewish state will never get off the ground." He raised his thick eyebrows in mirth. "And with an air force yet?"

"You mean your Uncle Joe might not approve of the matter?" Burt was referring to Stalin—Papa's hero—I guessed.

"Harry, a little poker later today?" inquired Mr. Ainbinder, who was brightly clad in a short-sleeved shirt.

"Thanks, Morris, not today."

Burt gave my head a little squeeze of affection. *Did my father see it?*

"By the way," my father said, taking my hand, "no more of this baseball foolishness for Aaron. He'll stay in school, if you don't mind."

Burt tilted his head slightly and seemed for a moment about to relent. Then he said, "You know what your trouble is, Harry? You live in America, not Russia, but you don't want to let Aaron grow up a native boy."

My chest pounded, and I felt my breathing quicken. Papa's face narrowed, and he paused for a few seconds in which he weighed the words and also the attention they might be attracting.

"I'll bring my son up my way, if you don't mind, again."

"Sure, Harry, sure." Burt backed off, shaking his head, giving up.

The sun reflected goldenly off the first-lieutenant bars on the shoulders of his short Eisenhower jacket, and I imagined him flying over Germany, piloting the B-17. When I had been told that Burt was a prisoner of war, I decided to write him a letter a week. I wrote to him about the Dodgers, our railroad, my new softball team. Week after week I went with my mother to the post office and mailed my letters to the air force in Washington, D.C. A Brigadier General John Hobson wrote back to me, saying that he would try his best to "forward on" my letters. His was on official U.S. government stationery, and I kept it carefully folded inside my private wooden box, made by Burt.

Mr. Werter interrupted. "C'mon, gents, instead of talking, how about a little arm wrestling? My boy is dying to see me getting licked."

"Yeah, take him on, Mr. Schlossberg," cried Steven. "Go ahead, teach him a lesson!" And he shook his own defeated hand vigorously before suckerpunching his father, who cuffed him back with an easy jab.

My father, smiling with embarrassment at the prospect of being drawn into the coarse action of the block, removed his suit jacket and allowed himself to be seated on a folding chair opposite Mr. Werter. Setting their elbows down upon a small, sturdy table, they locked grips and commenced, watched by a small group.

Knowing Papa's arm strength and his fierce pride, I was not at all surprised that he took up the challenge. I was also delighted that he and Burt were separated.

It didn't take long. By the time I could count to twenty, he had taken down Mr. Werter's arm to the squeals of his son and the surprise of the men. I myself felt both ways about it.

The four *kibbitzers* who had gathered around congratulated my father, who beamed at the acknowledgment and shook hands with Sol Werter.

My father was replacing his jacket, already standing, when Burt reappeared—from where I did not know. "Stay, Harry," he said. "I'll take you on."

Papa's eyes widened, then he smiled.

First loosening, then removing his tight khaki jacket, Burt took Mr. Werter's seat and got into position, his elbow placed solidly on the table and his hand up.

I put all my superstitious powers to work for Burt,

for me. I looked four times at the regular cracks in the sidewalk cement, counted to eight three times, and scratched at my kneecaps. The smallish crowd had increased, and encouragement was shouted to both sides.

At first I thought Burt could do it, and maybe so did he. He had gotten my father's hand down half-way with steady pressure, and it seemed just a matter of moments before he'd pin him. As I watched my father's face, the broad-bridged nose and hard, small eyes, I saw it fill with . . . determination. But just as Burt pressed down for the final pin, I saw some-thing else in my father's face: the bare hint of a smile. And I understood, then, that he had been playing a cruel game of deception with Burt. Slowly, he guided their hands into a reverse motion, forcing Burt's hand down toward the table, trying perhaps to squeeze something else out of him. Burt's face went that same ashen color I so feared, and I wanted to go to him, to bring him water the way I did at the Dodger games. But at least it was over.

"Come, another try?" my father offered, showing

apparent generosity. Cunning generosity, perhaps.

Burt, his mouth twitching slightly from the stress, forced himself to comply.

Don't, Burt, don't! I wanted to yell. But my tongue and my brain were frozen, cowardly frozen.

Once again, they put their arms and hands into a locked position, and at Sol's "one . . . two . . . three," got to work. Studying Burt's slender hand and wrist pressed against my father's thick wrist and hairy hand, I wondered if there was any chance in the world. I decided to test God, swearing a silent oath to believe in him, even to go to synagogue the following Saturday, if he'd help Burt win. But the same pattern emerged. Father allowed Burt the upper hand at the start, then moved him the other way, applying pressure slowly, slowly, as he observed the younger man's face. I hated his thick wrist covered with black hairs, and him, for his dirty cruelty. By the time Burt had been defeated again, he was ghostly pale and practically in tears as a result of the pain. My eyes were fixed on him, and I was unaware of my father or the crowd.

"Why didn't you tell us you were a *shtarker,* Herschel?" asked one of the men with new admiration.

I sneaked over to Burt's side and asked if he was all right. "Should I get you some water from the luncheonette?" I asked.

Smiling weakly, perspiring freely, he said, "Didn't do so well for us, did I, buddy?"

At that point, not caring what my father or the others thought, I buried my head in Burt's side, wetness exploding from my head and dissolving the scene.

DARKNESS ENVELOPED ME, except for the flickering of the screen. Later that afternoon, Russian soldiers in furry hats and long overcoats moved forward against a retreating Nazi army. Thick snow was falling, and gobs of it blanketed the trees, tanks, ground, and soldiers' uniforms. I recognized the music from my father's Soviet records, that deep patriotic chanting of the Red Army chorus. I sat low in my seat, huddled with my dizzying thoughts, despite my father's urgings to sit up straight. Gradually, however, in place of the somber chorus, I began to hear the cheerier sounds of Gladys's organ. And instead of the snowy war-front of the Russian steppes, I saw a green baseball diamond splashed with Brooklyn sunlight. Sure enough, there was Jackie— in white flannels with the Dodgers inscription in blue across his chest—leading off third. And as the pitcher went to his stretch, Robinson increased his lead step by step. Edging farther, farther from security, Jackie dared him to throw, either to third or to home, and finally the pitcher motioned his arm toward home. At that precise second there was Jackie. Racing. And hooksliding, away from the plate, he managed to reach out and touch home with his hand!

"What's wrong with you, silly boy?" my father whispered, causing me to jump. Placing his hand upon me with sudden tenderness, he asked, "Are you all right?" Then his strong hand cradled me to him, holding me there.

My heart, which had been whole with hostility, one with resentment, was crazily torn asunder, a condition that, I sensed—there in the shrouding, guilty darkness—would afflict me for a long, long time, if not forever.

THAT SUMMER, about the middle of July, my mother took me upstate to the mountains for our regular six-week vacation. We went up to White Sulphur Springs in the Catskills and stayed in a small hotel owned and run by a tough, piano-legged Hungarian widow. Because we had gone there the summer before, I had already made friends and could lose myself immediately in country pleasures. With the farmers' sons, I played hardball and helped with chores on the various dairy farms. With the other vacationing city kids, who stayed at nearby hotels or summer bungalows, I played softball and evening basketball, sneaked in to the nightly shows at the casinos, watched the waiters and busboys kidding with the girls. Sometimes one of the parents would take us on a small expedition to the town of Liberty, a half-hour drive, to the movies. Of course, these were very different from the sort of somber films I saw regularly with Father at the Stanley Theater in Manhattan. These were mostly light comedies or musicals.

Everything was green and lucid up there, in the

tree-filled hills where the air cooled off so aromatically at night, and the scent of pine and freshly cut hay cheered my dreams. And where I didn't have to face my father on a daily basis.

The Dodgers were doing real well, still heading the pack. I followed them on the radio, listening closely to Red Barber's funny descriptions and even odder southern drawl. Only he could call a fly ball to the outfield a "dying chicken falling out there in the pea patches" and make it sound like part of the game. Robinson was doing all right as well. There remained little question of his stamina, daring, or skill. In fact, he had become a hero to the fans of Brooklyn, despite the fact that some of his own players still resented him and opposing players were still out to get him. That's just too bad, we all thought . . . well, not all of us, as it turned out; I learned that quite a few of those farmers' kids were pretty prejudiced, and I got into two fistfights over my devotion to Jackie.

Burt, too, seemed to be doing fine. There were no more operations scheduled for the near future, so he was free to go to Palestine to fly planes for

the Jews. He was also seeing a woman pretty stead-
ily, a Czech lady who had been in the European
"camps" during the war. (Did that mean POW
camps, I wondered. Or was it the other kind I had
begun to learn about, in which the Nazi Germans
had murdered the Jews?) And when I kidded him
on the phone about "not getting married or anything dumb like that," he replied, "You never
know. But if I do, you'll be the first to hear about
it, pal. I'll need a best man, you know." After getting
Burt back from the war and the Nazis, the thought
of losing him that way pretty much knocked me
over!

I didn't think about Papa much, and he made it
easy by rarely coming up, always pleading work
duties. I really felt much freer and lighter without
him; life in the country held its own special routines
for me, and there didn't seem to be any need for my
father. So, when he'd ask me, over long distance,
whether I missed him or not, I was glad for the
fuzziness of the connection and uttered something
vague and meaningless. I suppose I didn't really take
his question or his sincerity seriously.

That's probably why I wasn't looking forward to the weekend in August when he was coming up for a visit.

And sure as shootin', an expression I used quite a bit that summer, my fears were fulfilled when he arrived. Papa wore his usual fall suit and tie as though he were still going to work or the club in the city. What a joke he was. I could see the hotel guests snicker behind his back on Saturday morning when, sitting outside in the wooden lawn chairs reading their newspapers, they spotted him. Oh, he was as polite as ever, polite and stiff, and I was embarrassed, almost ashamed to be seen with him. Although he was friendly, even warm, to me, I hardly gave him the opportunity to get close. I clearly saw the countryside as *my* territory, and he was out of place there. One thing though: his awkwardness gave me a feeling of revenge, even victory, you might say. It felt good.

That secret sense continued throughout the day and into the evening, when we went to see a show at the nearby Leona Hotel casino. We were entertained by a juggler, a comedian, and a singing act, and everyone in our group, including my mother and me, were having a fine time. Not Father. He watched politely enough, but didn't clap. Afterwards, when someone asked how he liked it, he raised his eyebrows.

"This *chazerai* you like? This crap!" he said to us privately. "Sometime, sonny boy, I'll take you to see a real juggler, and you'll see how fantastic it can be."

My mother's face tightened. "Sure, anything that we have *here* is not good enough for you. Do me a favor. Don't join us next time, yeah. Please."

And she went off to dance with a family friend, joining the crowd of people moving to the rumba music of the band. I watched her—auburn hair flying, hips moving, hands gesturing—at the center of the floor and was glad she was not going to let my father spoil her evening. Without his strict ways and European standards, my mother was freer, too.

The next morning my father disappeared after breakfast, and I prepared to go to a morning softball game. Gathering my glove and bat, I waited outside on the long wraparound porch for my friends to join me. The sun was bright and warm, and I hoped that by the time the game was over, it would almost be time for Papa to catch his bus home. Then we'd be free again.

However, just as my pals showed up, we heard a commotion on the large lawn adjoining the hotel and decided to see what was going on.

There was my father, sitting on a huge, chestnut-colored horse! Wearing leather riding boots and looking at home, he glanced around comfortably. Clusters of city vacationers, surprised and curious, had gathered to look at the beautiful animal that was grazing on the lawn. Papa was smiling, a different sort of smile than I had seen before, and I noticed drips of perspiration on his face as well as on the horse. Obviously, they had been riding hard.

Seeing me, he dismounted easily, and the crowd jumped back as the horse jerked his head and backed up a step. Papa merely stroked the horse's neck and said, "Sshhh. *Ess,* Red, *ess.*" Eat, Red, eat. "The clover is good, eh." Amazingly, the horse listened and began to graze once more. Red was a lovely reddish-brown color and had a white stripe down

his long head. His eyes were like big brown plums and seemed almost human.

Father wore his white shirt, but it was open at the neck, and he had rolled up his sleeves. He looked so different—not a stiff greenhorn, but a free and easy country fellow. Taking me around, he said, "So, sonny boy, how about a little ride?" He patted Red's broad but lean side. "He's a good *ferd*, this one."

The guests showed a new respect for Papa, putting hesitant, interested questions to him. Papa answered them in an easy, friendly manner. He was not aloof now, but relaxed.

My friend Joe Luftus asked, "Are you gonna ride him?"

I shrugged, trying to hide my excitement and fear.

Benjy Lewis added, "I didn't know your father was a real horseback rider. Why didn't you tell us?"

I smiled, not knowing what to say.

"Come," my father said to me, "I'll lift you up and then climb on myself."

Having no idea what was happening, I found myself hoisted up onto the saddle. Red turned lazily and gazed back at me—with doubt, I thought. Father whispered something to him and then, in one easy motion, lifted himself up behind me.

The crowd moved back, oohing and aahing, and my friends cried out encouragement to me. But I was so excited at just sitting there that I hardly understood their words. Everything looked so different from up there. The grown-ups were smaller, the kids shrimps, and the grassy ground dropped far below. The sky seemed closer, too.

My father showed me how and where to hold on to the saddle. Reins in hand, he touched Red with his heels, and the horse began to walk about. Around the lawn he, we, paraded, while everyone watched.

Just then my mother appeared, wearing an anxious expression. "You all right?" she asked me.

I nodded.

"Don't you go too fast with him," she warned my father.

I felt my father's strong arms around me, as he guided Red with gentle but firm hands. The horse seemed to understand perfectly his every command. After a few minutes, we proceeded outside the hotel's premises and onto the dirt shoulder of the road.

Leaning forward, Papa said, "Hold on now—we'll go a little faster." He made a little clicking sound, nudged the horse's sides, and I began to bounce up and down. It was a different experience—speedier, and a little scary. Up and down, up and down, the world bobbed by and my blood jumped, too.

At the end of a stretch of road, Papa pulled back on the reins, and we returned to a walk. He guided us across the empty blacktop to the grassy field opposite the hotel.

"How about a little gallop?" he asked, his face close. "All right, sonny?"

"Is it . . . much faster?"

"Sure."

"I'm afraid," I admitted, hating my fear. "Maybe we better not."

"Don't be silly. I have you, and he's a good horse."

"No," I said weakly—for I did want to try faster.

"First we'll just trot toward that farmhouse to make sure of the field," and he put Red onto his path.

I turned for a moment and saw the small crowd gathered by the hotel, observing, growing smaller and smaller, as we distanced ourselves from them. I thought of my friends watching, too, and tried to forget, or surmount, my fear.

When we were within about a hundred feet of the farmhouse, we turned. "Hold on!" Papa said, and he gave the horse a good kick with his boots.

With immediate thrust we took off, the ground beneath us disappearing suddenly. Red galloped as though he were flying, his hooves hardly touching the ground. Papa spoke words, but I was too scared to register their meaning and only felt his leaning body. I held on for dear life, tears in my eyes, my heart leaping. At some point I must have slipped to one side, because I felt my father's strong hand grab and right me with ease. It was like being on a train, traveling so fast that it was impossible to distinguish clearly the passing objects. Grassy fields, rows of trees, and an occasional white house were vanishing, while hotel, crowd, and road were approaching, no line separating the two. Exhilaration mingled with terror in my rushing blood.

We pulled up just short of the blacktop. Papa gave Red a loud pat on the neck, and then we walked back across the road. Papa's sweat fell on me, and I liked it.

Releasing my grip, I realized how tightly I had been clutching the saddle. My hands were sore, my heart was racing. Slowly, the ordinary world was returning to its right size.

My mother was furious, the hotel guests and my pals were cheering and clapping, and I felt my breathing return to normal.

Papa whispered to me, "Not too bad, eh, sonny boy?"

I had a surge of emotion, wanted even to hug and kiss him, but for some reason, I held myself back. Instead, I nodded, at a loss for words.

My father got down off the horse and asked someone the whereabouts of water. Red had already resumed his search for clover. Telling me he'd be right back, Papa asked whether I wanted to wait up there. Well, what could I say? Red grazed, I sat, and the grown-ups and kids surrounded me.

"How was it?"

"How'd ya stay on?"

"Do you know how fast you were traveling?"

"Was your dad in the cavalry or something?"

My mother anxiously asked, "Are you all right, Aaron?"

I nodded, said "fine," and, uncharacteristically, leaned away from her reaching hands.

My father returned with a bucket of water, and Red quickly turned his attention there. His nose submersed, he drank contentedly.

To father, my mother said, "*Bist du mishugah*. You scared the daylights out of me. How could you endanger the boy that way?"

But I knew differently; I knew something else.

Father made a weak gesture with his hands and gave Red a pat.

And I thought: Wouldn't it be great if Papa could take Red back home, to Brooklyn, where we could go out for rides with him all the time? He was a different man out there—with the horse, on roads and fields—and different with me, too. Why, he wouldn't always need to dream about his old house and old country; he could be happy right here. Then maybe he'd make America his home ground. Why, I could even take him out to see Jackie run and steal the bases!

Papa took me down from the horse, said he'd see me later, and got back on himself. "Time to go home, Red," he said, half smiling, wholly happy, and he walked the horse out of the lawn pasture.

Once on the road's shoulder, he kicked him lightly and prompted the horse back into that bumpy trot.

Everyone watched in rapt attention.

Benjy turned to me. "Boy, you're a lucky guy to have a pop who can ride like that. Where you been hiding him?"

The sun slanted down, camouflaging horse and rider in black shadow and greenish light. *Where you been hiding him?* The question repeated itself in my mind. Watching them both move down the road so easily and naturally, with athletic grace, I wondered the same thing.